Torera

by Monet Hurst-Mendoza

FOR PRODUCTION INQUIRIES

UNITED STATES AND CANADA
info@concordtheatricals.com
1-866-979-0447

UNITED KINGDOM AND EUROPE
licensing@concordtheatricals.co.uk
020-7054-7298

Each title is subject to availability from Concord Theatricals Corp., depending upon country of performance. Please be aware that *TORERA* may not be licensed by Concord Theatricals Corp. in your territory. Professional and amateur producers should contact the nearest Concord Theatricals Corp. office or licensing partner to verify availability.

This work is published by Samuel French, an imprint of Concord Theatricals Corp.

No one shall make any changes in this title(s) for the purpose of production. No part of this book may be reproduced, stored in a retrieval system, scanned, uploaded, or transmitted in any form, by any means, now known or yet to be invented, including mechanical, electronic, digital, photocopying, recording, videotaping, or otherwise, without the prior written permission of the publisher. No one shall share this title(s), or any part of this title(s), through any social media or file hosting websites.

For all inquiries regarding motion picture, television, online/digital and other media rights, please contact Concord Theatricals Corp.

MUSIC AND THIRD-PARTY MATERIALS USE NOTE

Licensees are solely responsible for obtaining formal written permission from copyright owners to use copyrighted music and/or other copyrighted third-party materials (e.g. artworks, logos) in the performance of this play and are strongly cautioned to do so. If no such permission is obtained by the licensee, then the licensee must use only original music and materials that the licensee owns and controls. Licensees are solely responsible and liable for clearances of all third-party copyrighted materials, including without limitation music, and shall indemnify the copyright owners of the play(s) and their licensing agent, Concord Theatricals Corp., against any costs, expenses, losses and liabilities arising from the use of such copyrighted third-party materials by licensees. For music, please contact the appropriate music licensing authority in your territory for the rights to any incidental music.

IMPORTANT BILLING AND CREDIT REQUIREMENTS

If you have obtained performance rights to this title, please refer to your licensing agreement for important billing and credit requirements.

TORERA was first produced by The Alley Theatre (Rob Melrose, Artistic Director; Dean R. Gladden, Managing Director) in Houston, Texas, and opened on May 17, 2023. The performance was directed by Tatiana Pandiani, with scenic design by Marcelo Martínez García, costume design by Rodrigo Muñoz, lighting design by Yuki Nakase Link, sound design by Yezminne Zepeda, projection design by Victoria Beauray Sagady, fight and intimacy direction by Adam Noble, and casting by Brandon Weinbrenner. Bullfighting consultation was provided by Olé Entertainment and Rodrigo Ortiz. The Production Stage Manager was Emily Bohannan and the Assistant Stage Manager was Laura Gutierrez. The cast was as follows:

ELENA MARÍA RAMÍREZ . . . . Jacqueline Guillén

TANOK CÁRDENAS . . . . Jesse Castellanos

PASTORA RAMÍREZ . . . . María Elena Ramírez

DON RAFAEL CÁRDENAS . . . . Eliud Garcia Kauffman

DANCERS/ENSEMBLE . . . . José José Arrieta Cuesta
and Carolína Ornelas

This play was made possible with support from The Public Theater's Emerging Writers Group, SPACE on Ryder Farm, Westport Country Playhouse, Long Wharf Theatre, and The Alley Theatre's 2022 Alley All New Festival.

CHARACTERS

ELENA MARÍA RAMÍREZ – Twelve to twenty-seven. Free-spirited, confident, unusually perceptive. Dreams of becoming a famous bullfighter. A great torera.

TANOK CÁRDENAS – Twelve to twenty-seven. A privileged, charming, slightly arrogant smart-ass but sweet-natured. A great rejoneador.

PASTORA RAMÍREZ – Early forties to fifties. Wise, loving, dutiful; mother to Elena, nanny and housekeeper to the Cárdenas family. Sharp and determined when needed.

DON RAFAEL CÁRDENAS – Late forties to fifties. A great rejoneador-turned-trainer in retirement; a taskmaster, dripping with machismo. Doesn't like to show emotion, but holds within him a suffocating vulnerability.

GROOMS/ENFERMERA/CUADRILLA TORERÉ/ENSEMBLE – TORERÉ in the bullring and stable helpers in the Picadero. The **ENFERMERA** can double with one of the **GROOMS**. Open to all gender identities.

SETTING

Various locations in Mexico – Mérida, Yucatán; Michoacán; Mexico City.

TIME

1992, 2002, 1987, 2007.

PLAYWRIGHT'S NOTES

Casting

Cast size can be flexible, depending on your needs. The number of Grooms/Toreré may vary, though I recommend having *at least* two.

All characters are to be played by Latiné actors, preferably Mexican or of Mexican descent if possible. Under no circumstances may these characters be portrayed by white actors, ever.

Language

/ indicates an interruption.

// indicates overlapping dialogue.

Staging

This play mimics a bullfight in its form. Please make every effort to stage in the round where possible.

The horses and bulls can be represented through various methods of stylized staging, from puppets to design to dancers, and beyond. Creativity and theatricality are highly encouraged, whatever your capabilities. For instance, in the world premiere at The Alley Theatre, ensemble dancers were used to represent the bull and horse, and also doubled as flamenco dancers for transitions. If you are using puppets to represent these animals, please utilize the Grooms to help ground the action in this world.

The play spans eighteen years. Elena, Tanok, Pastora, and Don Rafael will need to embody various ages during this timeframe. Please keep that in mind while crafting moments of physicality.

Music

The music in this play helps anchor us in time and emotional relevance. The songs act as another character, conveying beauty, joy, longing, and heartache. Each song was specifically chosen with this in mind. Please make every attempt to secure the rights to these works. If you are unable to do so, please choose alternate songs from the correct time period that carry the same emotional weight in their lyrics and thematically support the scenes in which they appear. If you're able to employ a talented musician to sing/play them live, go for it!

ACKNOWLEDGEMENTS

I am indebted and eternally grateful to the many humans who have made this work possible.

To Jesse Cameron Alick, Jack Phillips Moore, and my EWG cohort – your invaluable insights and creative input helped me sow the seeds for this play. It has blossomed beyond my wildest dreams. Thank you for your fellowship, support, and friendship.

To the entire staff at The Alley Theatre and my unbelievable cast and creative team, who made the world premiere of what I thought might be an unproducable play possible – your fearless embrace of every idea, strategy, prop, and design element was genuinely remarkable. I'm especially thankful for Liz Frankel, who was excited by this story from the beginning and brought it to the attention of artistic leadership, and for my conversations with Bradley Michalakis.

To my beautiful directors who have touched this play at various stages of its life – Elena Araoz, Katherine M. Carter, and Tatiana Pandiani. Thank you for being my second set of eyes, my closest confidants, my partners in crime. Your leadership styles and artistic visions, which are radical, exuberant, tireless, and a labor of pure love, have shaped this play into what it is today. You enhance everything you touch and are invaluable gifts to any playwright and the American Theater. (KMC: You are the first person I show anything I write to. I wouldn't be the storyteller I am without you.)

To Rodrigo Ortiz Barragan – thank you for sharing your love of this art form with everyone you meet. Your insights and expertise have brought authenticity and an infectious spirit to this work. Bullfighting is a cornerstone of our culture, and your reverence inspires open hearts and minds. There is more to it than meets the eye. Todo es toro.

To all the actors who have generously lent their time and talents to the creation of this play, including Jesse Castellanos, Maria Elena Ramirez, Eliud Garcia Kauffman, José José Arrieta Cuesta, Carolína Ornelas, Melissa Molano, Filipe Valle Costa, Juan Sebastián Cruz, Patricia Duran, Adriana Sananes, Sebastian Chacón, Juan Francisco Villa, Jose Antonio Melián, Oscar A. L. Cabrera, Julissa Roman, Coral Peña, Tony Plana, and Dakota Granados. Your exceptional performances and dedication to your craft have brought these characters to life and enriched this play in ways I could never have imagined.

To Jacqueline Guillén – thank you for always saying "yes" to me, no matter what crazy scenario I put you in. Your belief in me has been a constant source of strength and inspiration. Elena is who she is because you exist. You're more than my muse; you're my family. I can't wait to see what we create together as life continues.

To my agents, Beth Blickers and Nathan DeRemer, and my managers, Robert Lazar and Gerardo Machado – thank you for your guidance, negotiation skills, and the tireless efforts behind the scenes that have brought my career as a working writer to fruition.

To my mother, Cherilyn Hurst – thank you for instilling in me the conviction never to let my gender or financial status limit my dreams and for teaching me the value of perseverance in the face of opposition. You sacrificed so much so young so that my siblings and I could achieve despite numerous obstacles. You gave me wings to fly.

To my husband, Ugochukwu Anyanwu, who believes in me when I have trouble believing in myself. Your unwavering support, understanding, and love have been the bedrock of my creative journey. Thank you for plunging into the artistic depths alongside me and encouraging me to keep going, even when the end seems nowhere in sight. You are my anchor.

To the real-life toreras who inspired this journey – Conchita Cintrón, Lupita López, Cristina Sánchez, Karla de los Ángeles, and Conchi Ríos. You are icons. You are beauty, grace, and strength personified. You are the future.

And lastly, this play is dedicated to my grandparents, Beatríz and Ricardo Mendoza. You infused your adoration for Yucatán in me at an early age. You taught me how to love who I am and my ancestral line. You showed me the value of family in all its complicated and beautiful parts. My love for you is boundless, and I am profoundly proud to be your granddaughter.

Primer Tercio

**1.1 The Cárdenas Hacienda.
Mérida, Yucatán, México. 1992.**

(Dusk.)

(An orange grove. Seemingly hundreds of neat rows of orange trees with wild branches. The warm sunset kisses the tops of the green trees, creating shadows that make the tree trunks seem enormous. Eerie – like arms reaching out.)

(The scent of the fruit fills the theatre. The zest of the oranges should be so potent, it stings the nostrils of the patrons.)

(The sound of birds chirping gives way to the sound of hurried footsteps and children's laughter.)

ELENA. You're losing!

TANOK. You're *cheating*!

> *(****ELENA****, twelve, rushes on.)*

> *(****TANOK****, twelve, races after her. She's faster.)*

> *(They run around the stage, zig-zagging through the trees.)*

ELENA. *(Teasing.)* I thought you were the fastest man alive. Can't you catch me?

(**ELENA** *climbs a tree and hides from* **TANOK**.)

TANOK. *(Out of breath.)* Of course I can... I just...have a cramp...

I need to rest for a minute.

> *(As* **TANOK** *rests beneath the tree, struggling to catch his breath,* **ELENA** *appears above him. She slowly uncurls her body and dangles from the branch, like a snake.)*

ELENA. Giving up already? Is this the end of the great Tanok, only son of Yucatán's greatest rejoneador?

TANOK. Leave me alone!

ELENA. "En el nombre del Padre, del Hijo, y del Espíritu Santo... Dearly beloved: we are gathered here today to honor the memory of Tanok Cárdenas! He lived the way he ran: *S L O W L Y*."

TANOK. One day you're going to fall out of that tree.

> *(She stands on a sturdy branch with arms outstretched.)*

ELENA. Not possible. I'm a bird!

> *(She walks slowly across the branch, balancing.)*

TANOK. Mind your footing then, will you, palomita?

ELENA. I never fall. I'm invincible!

The wind is my friend, and together, we soar above everything!

TANOK. If you tear that dress, your mother will pull you by the ears and then my father'll blame me for starting trouble /

ELENA. Except nothing ever happens to you because they love you.

TANOK. It comes at a price. When you grow up, you'll see what I mean.

ELENA. Like you're so much older than me.

TANOK. Hey, six months is a long time!

Your problem is you still act like a child.

(She perches on the branch above him.)

ELENA. And *your* problem is that you want to be something more than what you are in this moment.

TANOK. It's called "responsibility," Elena.

You have a responsibility to your mother to be presentable for when the Governor arrives at this dinner tonight, and I have a responsibility to my father to keep the Cárdenas name in good standing.

(She climbs to a higher branch.)

ELENA. How ever do you sleep at night? So many worries for a such a pretty face.

TANOK. What about yours? Come down – te vas a romper la cara!

ELENA. Seriously, Tanok, relax. We came out here to be free.

TANOK. They're going to wonder where I am. Where *you* are.

ELENA. *(Gasp!)* Running around with your niñera's daughter? What will people say? Qué vergüenza!

TANOK. Exagerada.

ELENA. When I was swimming in my Mamá's belly, she was drying your tears and singing sweet songs into your ear.

A niñera is not just a nanny – she's your second mother.

How nice that you get *two*.

TANOK. That doesn't mean she loves you any less.

ELENA. That love comes at a price for me, too, Tanok.

You don't have to tell me about "responsibility" – it's already *expected* of me.

> *(Suddenly,* **ELENA** *loses her footing and slips. She screams.)*

TANOK.	**ELENA**.
Elena!	Tanok, help me!

> *(***TANOK*** *rushes to* ***ELENA***, *who is dangling from the high branch. She struggles to pull herself up.* ***TANOK*** *takes off toward the house.)*

TANOK. I'll go get Pastora!

ELENA. NO! My mother will pull my ears for climbing!

TANOK. I thought you weren't worried about her?

ELENA. OF COURSE I AM SHE'S MY MOTHER

Please! My feet are slipping!

TANOK. I'm underneath you. Just let go and I'll catch you.

ELENA. What if the breeze carries me a few degrees to your left and I crack my skull open and my brains dribble out?

TANOK. Aren't you friends with the wind?

ELENA. Friendships are fickle.

TANOK. Not ours.

ELENA. *(Struggling.)* Swear it!

TANOK. On my life, Elena, I swear I won't let your brains dribble out.

ELENA. OK... I'm letting go... uno, dos –

(Her fingers slip. She screams. She lands in
TANOK*'s arms. His legs buckle under the force*
of her weight, and they fall down together,
ELENA *on top of* **TANOK***.)*

TANOK. Ow.

ELENA. You actually caught me!

TANOK. I think you broke my leg. How many pan dulces
have you eaten today?

ELENA. Not as many as you, panzón.

(Patting his belly.)

You *do* make a nice cushion.

TANOK. You're like a hurricane that never goes away. If
you were any other girl /

ELENA. You'd try to kiss me?

(A moment. Then:)

ELENA. *(Playing it off.)*	**TANOK**.
"Ay, Tanok! Gracias por salvarme la vida!"	Ew! Gross! Not even if you were the last girl on Earth.

*(***ELENA*** bats her eyelashes maniacally at* **TANOK***, and pouts her lips. He playfully pushes her face away.)*

(A church bell tolls in the distance.)

TANOK. We should go back inside.

ELENA. But – la corrida.

TANOK. Maybe tomorrow. It's almost dinner time.

ELENA. You can be a few minutes late.

(From her dress pocket.)

ELENA. I brought my coin…

(She dangles the coin before **TANOK**. *He looks back at the house.)*

TANOK. And then we head back?

ELENA. As fast as we can.

(He considers.)

TANOK. Okay!

ELENA. Yes!

(She hands the coin to **TANOK**.*)*

TANOK. Heads or tails?

ELENA. Heads.

(He flips the coin. The big reveal in silence.)

(A shift. This is a ritual for them.)

*(***TANOK** *removes his vest and hands it to* **ELENA**. *They go to opposite ends of the grove.)*

TANOK. *(To audience, as* **ANNOUNCER**.*)* "Señoras y señores! Muchachos y muchachas! Introducing the bravest woman in all of México! As swift as the wind, as dazzling as the morning sun! The one, the only, Elena María Ramírez!"

*(***ELENA** *proudly waves to the audience, bows. She raises her invisible hat in the air to them. The corrida is about to begin. She takes her place, displaying Tanok's vest as a makeshift capote.)*

(To audience, as an announcer.) El Primer Tercio!

*(**TANOK** transforms into the bull. He scrapes the dirt with his "hooves" and uses his fingers to create fierce horns. He snorts.)*

ELENA. Ándale, toro!

*(**TANOK** charges. A clean sweep of the "capote" as he passes through the fabric.)*

(Again from a new angle.)

(Calling the "bull.") Hey! Hey!

*(**TANOK** charges her, she makes the pass.)*

(Again. Call, charge, pass with a flourish.)

TANOK. *(To audience, as **ANNOUNCER**.)* El Segundo Tercio!

*(**ELENA** breaks off two nearby branches to act as her banderillas.)*

*(She calls the bull again. As **TANOK** and **ELENA** charge one another, she lands the "banderillas" with a flourish in the middle of his back. He slows, pretends to be weakened.)*

*(**ELENA** addresses an invisible "guest of honor" in the crowd.)*

ELENA. "Señora Presidenta!"

TANOK. *(Breaking character.)* "Señora Presidenta?"

ELENA. *(Breaking character.)* Woman matador, woman president.

TANOK. Fair enough.

(They resume.)

ELENA. "Señora Presidenta! With your permission, I'd like to conclude La Fiesta. In your honor, it would be my pleasure to slay this noble bull."

TANOK. *(As President, exaggerated high-pitch.)* By the power vested in me, you may slay this beast, and we shall rejoice!

> *(He takes out a handkerchief and waves it, imitating the crowd cheering wildly.)*

ELENA. *(To* **TANOK***, with reverence.)* Tercer Tercio.

> *(***ELENA*** takes one of the "banderilla" branches, puts it through the sleeves of Tanok's vest to create her make-shift muleta.)*

> *(***ELENA*** and* **TANOK** *take their positions once more. She calls the bull, emulates three clean passes with her "muleta." Even at twelve, we see her skill and reverence for the art. She removes the branch from the vest, holds it proudly in the air.)*

And now my sword! La estocada!

> *(***ELENA*** gets uncomfortably close to* **TANOK***, who is hunched over on the ground before her. She strokes his hair. She speaks into his ear:)*

Thank you for the dance, Toro Bravo!

> *(With grace and ferocity,* **ELENA** *delivers a single sword thrust through the nape of the neck, severing the spinal column.* **TANOK** *collapses. The bull is now dead.)*

> *(After a moment,* **TANOK** *rises to his feet. He raises* **ELENA***'s arm into the air and shows her off to the invisible crowd.)*

TANOK. *(To audience, as an announcer.)* Viva, Elena María Ramírez! La Torera!

> (**ELENA** *bows reverently. Celebration! He hands her an orange.)*

For your victory. You honor all of México with your bravery!

ELENA. Gracias. Viva, México!

TANOK. Viva!

> *(They collapse on the ground with laughter. The game is over.)*

Not bad! Your capework is the best it's ever been!

ELENA. I've been watching Ignacio de la Vega on TV.

TANOK. *(Apprehensive.)* He's so flashy! Did you see him on his knees doing the Porta Gayola?

ELENA. *(Thrilled.)* It's like he's not afraid of anything. I want to be like that one day!

TANOK. Well, keep this up and maybe you will be.

ELENA. Tanok, you really think so?

TANOK. If Conchita Cintrón could do it, why can't you?

ELENA. Because Conchita Cintrón *owned* horses – which means she had money, which means people loved her, which means she was noticed. I'm invisible.

TANOK. *(Sincere.)* I see you, palomita.

ELENA. Have you ever just felt that you were born to do something, Tanok?

Like you couldn't control it? That's how I feel about the corrida.

The spectacle, the dance!

When Ignacio de la Vega is in the bullring, it's like there's nothing else in the world.

ELENA. Just him and the Toro Bravo.

And then, right before the gate opens, you realize the veil between life and death is so thin. Just one mistake can tear it – in that moment, *that* is the only truth there is.

>   *(Beat.)*

Can you imagine? La Plaza de Toros México! It must be so beautiful. The crowds screaming your name as you walk through the streets, the band playing a pasodoble as you step into the ring. Being the pride and joy of Yucatán.

>   *(A moment as they visualize this shared dream.)*

You're so lucky you get to train on horseback.

You're going to be a great rejoneador when you grow up, Tanok – just like your father.

TANOK. "Just like my father."

The other day, I tried to charge Gitana during practice and she got spooked. I fell and he told me he'd seen more promise from a blind cripple.

>   *(**TANOK** is defeated, but **ELENA** springs into action to comfort him.)*

ELENA. So, we'll practice more!

After dinner, we'll run to the stables. You can ride Gitana, and I can be the Toro Bravo for *you*!

>   *(She mimes being the bull and prepares to charge **TANOK**. She chases him, before tackling him to the ground. They giggle and wrestle around until **ELENA** gains the upper hand. She straddles **TANOK**, pins him down.)*

You're dead. You've got to be quicker than that!

TANOK. You're my best friend, Elena.

When I am a famous rejoneador, I'll take you to the Plaza with me.

ELENA. Not if I get there first!

> *(Elena's mother, **PASTORA**, calls out to them in the distance.)*

PASTORA. *(Offstage.)* Elena! Tanok! Entren ya /

TANOK. Your mother's calling.

> *(**ELENA** and **TANOK** separate immediately, like a teenage couple busted by their parents.)*

PASTORA. *(Offstage.)* Vamos a cenar!

TANOK. *(Pulls leaf out of **ELENA**'s hair.)* Look at you – a mess!

> *(**ELENA** offers her pinky.)*

ELENA. *(A proposal.)* One way or another, we take each other to the Plaza.

TANOK. On my life.

> *(They interlock pinkies – deal made.)*

Tag, you're it!

> *(**TANOK** takes off running. **ELENA** follows.)*

> *(Lights.)*

1.2 A Dreamscape.

(The **ENSEMBLE DANCERS** *enter the dreamscape as a bull and horse. Their movements mimic both animals and humans, as they move through various steps of the corrida.)*

*(***ELENA** *enters in her school uniform, and we realize this is her daydream. She makes eye contact with the "bull" and uses her skirt as a capote. The bull passes through the fabric, running offstage.)*

*(The kitchen moves in. ***ELENA** *grabs two large spoons off the counter and practices with them as banderillas.)*

*(***PASTORA** *enters, breaking the dreamscape.)*

PASTORA. Elena! Apúrate!

(We snap into reality.)

(Lights.)

1.3 The Cárdenas Hacienda. 1992. Kitchen.

(Early morning light spills through the windows. A rooster crows.)

*(On the stove, beans boil and rice cooks. A batch of pre-made tortillas sit in a tortilla warmer on the counter. **PASTORA** takes a pan of sautéed onions off the fire.)*

PASTORA. *(To **ELENA**.)* The sun's coming up. Crack those eggs into this pot.

> *(**ELENA** does as she's told while **PASTORA** kneads masa. Her movements are swift and firm – beautiful violence. As the women work away in silence, the sounds of their chores fill the kitchen like a symphony.)*

Remember, don't add /

ELENA. Salt.

PASTORA. Muy bien, mi niña.

Y el café?

ELENA. In the dining room.

> *(Handing her mother the pot.)*

Eggs.

PASTORA. I want to show you something – How to make the perfect egg:

Hold your hand over the burner. Wait until it's nice and hot.

> *(**ELENA** holds her hand over the stove. When it's hot enough:)*

ELENA. Ouch!

PASTORA. That means it's ready.

> *(In real time, **PASTORA** helps her daughter cook the eggs – a seamless combination of demonstration and hand-over-hand.)*

Put the pot on the fire, and lower the heat just a bit so it doesn't burn.

Add a sliver of butter. This makes the eggs taste like clouds.

Don't ever stop stirring the eggs as they cook – your arm should feel like it's going to fall off.

Now, take the pot off the heat...

> *(**ELENA** does. Her arm weakens and she nearly stops stirring.)*

But keep stirring!

Do that a few times – on the heat, stir; off the heat, stir.

When the eggs are nice and light, turn off the burner and add a spoonful of crema.

This cools the eggs so that they don't overcook in the pan.

> *(**PASTORA** adds the sautéed onions to the mix.)*

Now the onions – it adds extra flavor.

Don't let any oil from the pan drip into the pot.

The salt comes last – any earlier makes the eggs too watery, and all your hard work will be for nothing.

> *(**PASTORA** feeds **ELENA** a spoonful of the eggs.)*

Well?

ELENA. Mmmm! They're perfect!

PASTORA. Being exact and being creative are one and the same.

Set out their plates.

> (**ELENA** *sets out three ornate plates in an assembly line on the table, as* **PASTORA** *folds tortillas into elegant triangular shapes and plates them.*)

I'll fold the tortillas. What's next?

ELENA. Rice?

PASTORA. Mhmm.

> (**ELENA** *grabs the pot of rice off the stove and scoops it onto the plate, next to the tortillas.*)

Carefully – only serve what will be eaten.

Beans next, but in the /

PASTORA.	**ELENA**.
Little bowls.	Little bowls.

> (**ELENA** *scoops the beans into three small bowls from the same flatware set, and places them on the plate.*)

PASTORA. Bien hecho, amor.

You can sprinkle a little cheese on top of the beans if you have any.

> (*A shared secret.*)

I always do.

> (**ELENA** *smiles, as* **PASTORA** *sprinkles queso fresco over the beans.*)

And finally, the egg.

*(**ELENA** plates the egg.)*

PASTORA. Buenisimo, Elena! You'll make a wonderful wife one day.

Now, take those into the dining room for Doña Beatríz and Don Rafael.

> *(**ELENA** exits into the dining room area with two plates.)*

> *(**PASTORA** serves the remaining food on two ordinary plates for herself and **ELENA**. The food isn't divided, no special presentation. She sets the plates down on the kitchen table and begins to manually juice the oranges.)*

> *(Behind her, **TANOK** stealthily sneaks into the kitchen, also in uniform.)*

> *(He moves to silently grab a pan dulce from a plate on the kitchen table.)*

> *(Without turning her back:)*

Hands off. That pan dulce's for later.

TANOK. How did you know it was me?

PASTORA. I have eyes in the back of my skull. I know everything you do, always.

TANOK. I thought only God knew everything.

PASTORA. When it comes to you, I have God's eyes.

> *(**PASTORA** pulls out a bowl, covered by a napkin.)*

Mira: tu favorito.

> *(She pulls off the napkin, revealing cut papaya.)*

TANOK. Papaya! Con sal y limón?

PASTORA. Claro! What kind of niñera would I be if I didn't know you better than you know yourself?

TANOK. Gracias, Mamita.

PASTORA. Anything for you, mi vida.

> *(She hands him his plate of eggs, rice, and beans and the papaya. **ELENA** re-enters, as **TANOK** kisses **PASTORA** lovingly on the cheek. **PASTORA** resumes cleaning the kitchen.)*

ELENA. *(With sass.)* That one's poisoned.

> *(**TANOK** playfully sticks his tongue out at her. She blows a raspberry at him.)*

PASTORA. Ay, dejen de hacer tonterías! Breakfast is getting cold. Sit down and eat. Now.

ELENA.   **TANOK**.
Sí, Mamá.   Sí, Mamita.

> *(**ELENA** takes her seat at the kitchen table. **TANOK** starts to exit toward the dining room. **PASTORA** listens to the following exchange while she busies herself in the kitchen.)*

ELENA. *(To **TANOK**.)* So, what do you think? Twenty minutes and then we can start walking?

TANOK. Oh…sorry, Elena…my father said he'd drive me.

> *(**ELENA** looks up from her breakfast and stares at him.)*

ELENA. *(Matter of fact.)* But it's Thursday.

We always walk to school together because you don't have to train on Thursday mornings.

TANOK. I know, but I can't today.

ELENA. Why is he driving you? He never takes you to school.

TANOK. *(Lying.)* I guess today he wants to. It's not that big a deal.

ELENA. Were you even going to say something to me?

TANOK. I'm telling you now.

> *(Uncomfortable silence.* **ELENA** *is obviously upset, but tries to hide it. When* **TANOK** *can't take it anymore:)*

I'm going to the tentadero with my father to see the bulls for Saturday's corrida, okay?

He says if I want to be a great rejoneador, I need to see how big and strong they can be.

I didn't tell you because I didn't want to hurt your feelings.

ELENA. *(Guarded.)* Why would that hurt my feelings?

> *(***TANOK*** *says nothing.)*

You can't just be late for school.

TANOK. Well, he thinks this is more important.

PASTORA. *(Diffusing.)* Elena – Tanok has things to do and so do you.

Go on, Tanok.

> *(As* **TANOK** *starts to leave.)*

ELENA. *(To* **TANOK**.*)* Must be nice to just do whatever you want, whenever you want.

TANOK. See? This is why I didn't tell you. You're acting all weird now.

ELENA. I'm not! I just don't get why you didn't tell him you have other plans.

TANOK. What would I even say?

"Perdóname, señor, but Elena says I have to walk her to school today."

ELENA. That sounds pretty good.

TANOK. Rafael Cárdenas has never heard "no" from anyone his entire life.

ELENA. *(Piecing it together.)* Wait… You actually *want* to go.

TANOK. Yes, Elena! *I* want to go!

(This stings more than **ELENA** *would like it to.)*

ELENA. Oh. Then I guess that's that.

TANOK. You can still come watch me and Gitana practice after school.

I have some allowance left – we can go to El Colón after and get sorbetes.

ELENA. *(Pointedly.)* Yeah, sure. That sounds fun.

TANOK. Are you mad?

ELENA. No.

TANOK. You *are* mad.

ELENA. Aren't you late for breakfast? Shouldn't you be sitting in the *other* room with your father instead of in the kitchen talking to me?

(This strikes a nerve in **TANOK**. *He exits to the dining room.)*

(When he's gone, **ELENA** *angrily eats her food.* **PASTORA** *joins* **ELENA**.*)*

PASTORA. That wasn't very fair, pollita.

ELENA. You're always taking his side! You're *my* Mamá – you're supposed to defend *me*!

PASTORA. And I do – but you have to know your place, Elena.

You may be Tanok's friend, but Don Rafael is his *father*. He has the final word on everything. Tanok has to respect him, just like you have to respect me.

ELENA. Tanok *lied* to me, Mamá.

PASTORA. He did the right thing in not telling you. A girl has no place being near those wild animals.

ELENA. But, they're not wild! They're in a tentadero!

PASTORA. *(Firm.)* It doesn't matter where they are. It's dangerous, and I don't want you playing around there. Se acabo!

ELENA. Don Rafael ruins everything!

PASTORA. *(Sharp.)* Cállate! Don Rafael is the reason that you have a roof over your head and clothes on your back. So you will show him some respect and watch how you speak in this house, no matter how upset you are. Entiendes?

ELENA. Sí, Mamá.

PASTORA. I raised you to be free-spirited, but not *that* free-spirited.

> (**ELENA** *hangs her head low.*)

Mira, niña: Don Rafael has a very specific...*plan* for Tanok.

Their lives are consumed by risk and chance, but ours don't have to be.

Our place is here at home – to *support* them.

> *(Beat.)*

You and Tanok are growing up, Elena, and you will have different paths in your life.

Sometimes you will walk together – as friends – but you will also have to learn to walk alone.

ELENA. But I don't want to walk alone – especially on a Thursday!

PASTORA. Ay, mi vida, you're so very young still. In time, you'll understand what I mean.

(**ELENA** *doesn't respond.*)

I'll tell you what – I know something better than a tentadero that we can do together after school.

ELENA. *(Excited.)* Really?

PASTORA. Something special, maybe even a little wild...

(Hushed.)

Make marquesitas!

ELENA. Cheese and caramel make you fat and I need to be able to run fast. I can't eat those anymore, Mamá.

PASTORA. You are beautiful the way you are, Elena.

Besides, a girl with an appetite has strong hips, and strong hips mean healthy children. And when you have children, you'll always be running, whether you're fat or not. So, come home after school and *eat*.

(**ELENA** *quickly gets up and puts her dish in the sink.* **PASTORA** *hands* **ELENA** *her lunch.*)

ELENA. I gotta go.

PASTORA. Straight home, okay?

(**ELENA** *kisses her mother and scurries out the door.*)

*(Finally alone, **PASTORA** sits at the kitchen table, ready to eat. She bows her head and prays silently. As she brings a spoonful of food to her mouth:)*

DON RAFAEL. *(Offstage.)* Pastora, necesitamos más café! Pastora!

(She puts her utensil down and exits into the dining room with a coffee pot. The kitchen is finally still as Pastora's hot breakfast sits untouched on the table.)

(Lights.)

1.4 The Cárdenas Hacienda. 1992.
The Picadero (Riding Hall)

(Afternoon.)

*(**TANOK** is mounted atop a majestic steed, Gitana, bareback. They make steady trots around the ring, as **DON RAFAEL** stands in the center of the ring, arms crossed, watching.)*

DON RAFAEL. Remember to pull your hips up… Take some of the weight off her every once in a while. Back straight!

*(**TANOK** adjusts.)*

Better.

How are your balls?

TANOK. Sore.

DON RAFAEL. Good.

If you can master your balance and maintain your strength while riding bareback, you'll lower your chances of getting yourself killed in the ring.

Too many riders use their saddle and reins as a crutch. In the corrida, *you* have to be in control.

Back *straight*, goddamn it!

TANOK. I need a break!

DON RAFAEL. You'll rest when I say you can.

TANOK. My legs are shaking!

DON RAFAEL. Quitter! Do you want this or not?

TANOK. I do.

DON RAFAEL. Then, be a man! If you want a place at the top, you'll have to earn it.

DON RAFAEL. Focus – push yourself!

> (**TANOK** *adjusts, and trots around once more with fervor.*)

Better.

Now, turn her...

> (**TANOK** *uses his heels to tell Gitana which way to move.*)

Head up!

> (**TANOK** *lifts his head. For a moment, time stops. The world becomes warmer, and the soft sounds of a roaring crowd echo throughout the ring.*)

> (**TANOK** *breathes deeply, and smiles. He waves to the invisible crowd, and for the first time, we see a grace and charisma pour out of* **TANOK** *that we've never seen before. He's actually perfect for this life.*)

> (*Then:*)

Ya – enough!

> (*The fantasy is broken, and* **TANOK** *is snapped back into reality.*)

Bring her in.

> (**DON RAFAEL** *moves to the edge of the ring and pulls out a few carrots.* **TANOK** *dismounts, leads Gitana to* **DON RAFAEL**, *who hands* **TANOK** *the treats.*)

Reward her.

> (**TANOK** *feeds Gitana the carrots.*)

You want to keep her happy. She won't go to battle for you otherwise.

> (**DON RAFAEL** *caresses the horse with a soft brush.*)

It takes many years to high-school a horse successfully. You must not only possess great skill, but you must also have a greater understanding of equine mentality.

> (*Handing* **TANOK** *the brush.*)

You have to know where and how to touch her, and make it precise, so that she knows exactly what you need her to do; she is an extension of your body.

> (*Gitana nuzzles* **TANOK** *gently as he brushes her.* **TANOK** *kisses her.*)

You and Gitana are truly quite a pair.

Rejoneo is an art. I only push you because I know you can be a great artist, Tanok. When the time comes, you will be invincible.

TANOK. I hope so, Señor.

DON RAFAEL. Of course you will. You're my son.

I wouldn't expect anything less.

> (**DON RAFAEL** *grabs a small wooden stool and a riding crop.*)

You're improving. So, how about a game?

TANOK. *(Brighter.)* You mean it?

DON RAFAEL. You *might* be ready to move on from trotting. Let's see if I'm right.

> (**TANOK** *looks up to the tribuna for* **ELENA**, *but she isn't there.*)

Who are you looking for?

TANOK. No one.

DON RAFAEL. She's not allowed here.

TANOK. I just had something in my eye.

Please, Señor, what's next?

DON RAFAEL. Time to test your precision.

Get on Gitana and go to the other end of the ring.

> (**TANOK** *does as he's told.*)

Hold this.

> (**DON RAFAEL** *hands* **TANOK** *the riding crop and moves into the center of the ring. He reveals the stool and draws a large "X" on it with chalk. Gitana prances around excitedly.*)

This stool is the bull.

That riding crop is your banderilla.

On my signal, you gallop toward me and I'll charge at you.

Get as close as you possibly can.

If you can land your "banderilla" on this "X," you win.

If I touch Gitana, you lose.

> (**TANOK** *gets into position. He looks up to the tribuna again.* **ELENA** *still isn't there.*)

Tanok!

TANOK. I'm ready, Señor.

DON RAFAEL. Wait for the signal.

> (**TANOK** *whispers into Gitana's ear and gently pats her mane. When ready,* **DON RAFAEL** *gives the signal.* **TANOK** *kicks*

Gitana and she jolts forward towards the stool. **TANOK** *raises himself up, and hoists the riding crop to strike, as* **DON RAFAEL** *moves forward.* **TANOK** *misses and* **DON RAFAEL** *hits his leg with the chair – hard and with intention – knocking* **TANOK** *off Gitana and into the ring.)*

*(***TANOK*** *rolls over, hurt. He breathes heavily.* **DON RAFAEL** *stands over him.)*

You lose.

TANOK. I'm sorry.

DON RAFAEL. En la corrida es matar o morir. There's no room for distraction.

(Beat.)

I misjudged you.

*(***DON RAFAEL*** *throws him a towel.)*

Clean yourself up. That's all for today.

(He begins to walk away. **TANOK**, *winded, tries to stand on his feet with great difficulty.)*

TANOK. Let me try again. I – I can get it right.

DON RAFAEL. Another time, perhaps. When you're *ready*.

TANOK. Papá – wait!

*(***DON RAFAEL*** *exits.)*

*(***TANOK*** *is left alone in the ring.)*

(He looks around the stands for the invisible crowd – for **ELENA** *– but there is no one.)*

(Lights.)

1.5 The Cárdenas Kitchen. 1992.

(Late afternoon.)

*(***PASTORA*** *dances around the kitchen, humming to a Vaquería song on the radio.*[*]* *The music emanates from everywhere in the kitchen – the window, the floor, the sink, the stove – and blooms like a flower.)*

*(***ELENA***, at the stove, makes marquesitas. Her books/homework sits open on the kitchen table.)*

PASTORA. When I was a little girl, I would stand on this kitchen table and stamp like a Vaquería dancer en La Plaza Grande.

Tap-tap-tap-stomp! Tap-tap-tap-stomp!

Mamí hated that. She would get so furious!

(As her mother.)

"Pastora! Qué haces encima de mi mesa?!" These little divots are from my heels.

Tap-tap-tap-stomp! Tap-tap-tap-stomp!

For your abuelita, the kitchen was for working with your hands to serve others – but for me, it was my private stage.

Every part of it sang to me, and when I hear music, I can't help but dance.

From then on, the kitchen was my favorite room in this entire house.

---

[*] A license to produce *Torera* does not include a performance license for any third-party or copyrighted music. Licensees should create an original composition or use music in the public domain. For further information, please see the Music and Third-Party Materials Use Note on page iii.

The kitchen is where you *create*.

The kitchen is where you are your truest self.

You compose happiness here – for yourself, for others.

And it all starts with a table.

ELENA. You should ask Don Rafael for a new one. This one gives me splinters.

PASTORA. Your abuelita used to nurse Don Rafael right here – I don't think he could part with this table anymore than I could.

> (**PASTORA** *caresses the wooden table, thinking fondly of the memories it has seen over the years.*)

Oh, the secrets she could tell.

> (*She rests her ear against it.*)

Listen.

> (**ELENA** *follows her mother's lead.*)

ELENA. I don't hear anything.

PASTORA. She's quiet today. But, one day, you too will hear la música.

> (**PASTORA** *closes her eyes and caresses the table, remembering.*)

ELENA. Mamá?

PASTORA. Sí, cielito?

ELENA. Did you ever play with Don Rafael when you were little?

PASTORA. All the time.

> (**PASTORA** *moves to the stove, resumes cooking.*)

ELENA. Are you still friends?

> (**PASTORA** *doesn't answer, drizzles caramel onto her marquesita.*)

Well?

PASTORA. Well, what?

ELENA. Are you?

PASTORA. *You* are my best friend now.

ELENA. That doesn't count!

PASTORA. Of course it does. You are everything to me.

ELENA. But, who do you talk to about grown-up things?

PASTORA. *(Half-beat.)* God.

> (**PASTORA** *takes a bite of her marquesita.*)

Mmm! Deliciosa!

> (**ELENA** *takes a bite. She tries to only eat one because it's so decadent, but can't help herself. She gobbles it down.* **PASTORA** *smiles.*)

So, did you and Tanok work things out?

ELENA. No.

PASTORA. You will. That boy adores you.

ELENA. He makes me want to vomit.

PASTORA. You don't mean that.

ELENA. I do!

PASTORA. Elena, you two are fused together at the heart.

Sometimes your hearts become so full you'll scream until your lungs give out and cry until your eyes feel like the desert.

But when two hearts are fused together like yours and Tanok's, they become elastic.

No matter how much they bend and twist and stretch, eventually they always come back to one another – as friends.

> *(Beat. Then:)*

ELENA. Well, we won't! I won't speak to that carifeo for as long as I live!

> *(***TANOK*** *enters the kitchen, filthy from practice.)*

PASTORA. *(Aside, to* **ELENA.***)* As long as you live, eh?

TANOK. Hola, Mamita.

PASTORA. Hola, precioso.

> *(***TANOK*** *hugs* **PASTORA,** *making eye contact with* **ELENA** *over her shoulder.)*

TANOK. *(Pointedly.)* Elena.

> *(He picks up the segment of a peeled orange off the counter, looks right at* **ELENA** *and sucks on it loudly.* **ELENA** *retorts, sucking on another segment, staring* **TANOK** *dead in the eyes. The two parry back and forth, making loud, obnoxious eating sounds. The action crescendos when* **TANOK** *and* **ELENA** *grab cloth napkins off the table and start whipping each other. When* **PASTORA** *can't take it anymore:)*

PASTORA. Ay, this is ridiculous! I won't have my children fighting!

ELENA. He's not even yours!

TANOK. Don't shout at her!

PASTORA. Basta!

>　(**TANOK** *and* **ELENA** *stop immediately.*)

I did not raise you to act like beggars arguing in the streets.

You have a warm home, food on the table, and arms to hold you – bendito sea Dios.

You two are my soul and I love you *both*, so get used to it.

And you love *each other* – get used to that, too.

(To **TANOK.***)* Tanok, you lied to Elena.

TANOK. I didn't want to make her upset!

PASTORA. Life is upsetting. Your intentions to keep her safe are very sweet, but completely misguided. You want to be a good friend? Be honest.

(To **ELENA.***)* And Elena – you hurt Tanok's feelings today.

ELENA. How?!

PASTORA. You weren't very understanding.

TANOK. *And* she didn't come to my practice!

ELENA. *(To* **TANOK.***)* I don't have to if I don't want to!

TANOK. You said you'd be there!

ELENA. No, I didn't!

TANOK. You said it sounded "fun"!

ELENA. Ever heard of "sarcasm"?

TANOK. I fell off my horse looking for you. It's all your fault!

ELENA. *(Baby-voice.)* Ay, pobrecito, el bebito...

>　(**PASTORA** *pulls their ears.*)

ELENA & TANOK. Ooooowwwwwwww!

PASTORA. Apologize to one another.

> (**ELENA** *and* **TANOK** *are silent, enduring the pain while trying to outlast the other.*)

I can wait.

> (**TANOK** *finally gives in from the pain.*)

TANOK. Okay, okay – perdón! I'm sorry I lied to you, Elena.

I was trying to do the right thing, but I hurt your feelings instead.

> (*Beat.*)

ELENA. Good!

> (**PASTORA** *pulls* **ELENA**'s *ear harder.*)

Owwww! Okay, okay!

(*To* **TANOK**.) I'm sorry, too. I just...don't like you changing our plans.

> (**PASTORA** *lets them go.*)

TANOK. (*Sincerely.*) I'm not going to leave you behind.

"One way or another," remember?

> (**ELENA** *softens. They rush to embrace each other.*)

PASTORA. There. You see? Fused at the heart.

> (*A service bell on the kitchen wall rings.*)

Tanok, your mother needs me. Leave those dirty clothes in the washroom. Elena, start chopping the vegetables for dinner. Ya es tarde.

(*Aside, to* **ELENA**.) Pórtate bien – remember who you are.

(**PASTORA** *exits.*)

(When she's out of sight, **TANOK** *pulls* **ELENA** *aside.)*

TANOK. I have a surprise for you. I'm taking you to the corrida with me on Saturday.

ELENA. *(Excited.)* Really?! I've never been to an actual corrida before!

(Reality sets in.)

But wait... What about your father?

TANOK. Once he starts talking to his old bullfighting friends, it's like I'm not even there.

We can do whatever we want.

When Pastora leaves for the market, just come to the Plaza. I'll sneak down to the front and let you in. It'll be easy.

*(***ELENA*** thinks on this.)*

ELENA. If we get caught, my mother will give us the beat down of our lives.

TANOK. I'm game. Are you?

*(***ELENA*** smiles.)*

ELENA. Meet you there at three.

(They pinky promise.)

*(***TANOK*** exits toward the washroom, discarding his dirty clothes along the way. ***ELENA*** sits at the table and begins to chop the vegetables, smiling ear to ear. She squeals with delight.)*

(Lights.)

1.6 The Cárdenas Kitchen. 1992.

(Very late, that same night.)

(Moonlight spills through the open window. The gentle chirp of crickets gives way to a song in the style of "Piensa En Mi" by Chavela Vargas softly playing on the radio.[*])

(For once, there is stillness in this room – except for **PASTORA**, *who sits at the kitchen table sewing a hole in a pair of Rafael's trousers. Though her body is visibly tired, her spirit shines bright as she works, humming along to the song. There is nothing she'd rather be doing at this exact moment.)*

*(***DON RAFAEL*** appears in the doorway behind her, and watches* **PASTORA** *with great tenderness. For a brief moment, we get a glimpse of another life that could have been.)*

*(***DON RAFAEL*** moves to speak, but thinks better of it and exits instead.)*

*(***PASTORA*** looks up, as if she felt him standing there all along – but she just keeps on sewing and humming.)*

(Lights.)

---

[*] A license to produce *Torera* does not include a performance license for "Piensa En Mi" by Chavela Vargas. The publisher and author suggest that the licensee contact ASCAP or BMI to ascertain the music publisher and contact such music publisher to license or acquire permission for performance of the song. If a license or permission is unattainable for "Piensa En Mi," the licensee may not use the song in *Torera* but should create an original composition in a similar style or use a similar song in the public domain. For further information, please see the Music and Third-Party Materials Use Note on page iii.

Segundo Tercio

2.1 The Picadero. 2002.

(Very late.)

*(***TANOK*** [now wearing a medallion] leans against the wooden barrera, smoking a cigarette, waiting for* ***ELENA***. *Beside him on a stool are capped practice horns, his capote, muleta, and killing and aluminum swords.)*

*(***ELENA***, in a cleaning uniform, rushes on with a duffle bag. They attempt to remain inconspicuous/quiet.)*

ELENA.	**TANOK.**
Sorry, sorry, sorry!	You're late.

ELENA. The bus broke down so I had to walk.

*(***ELENA*** changes into her workout clothes. ***TANOK*** turns away to give her privacy.)*

TANOK. Anyone see you come in?

ELENA. Don't think so. What time will your father get here?

TANOK. Dawn. We have a few hours.

*(***TANOK*** steals a glance at ***ELENA***, against his better judgement. Noticing her beauty, he turns away again.)*

You shouldn't be walking back this late. I would've sent a car to go get you.

ELENA. I didn't have change to call you.

(Re: the cigarette.)

That'll kill you, you know.

(She takes a drag of it, and passes it back to him.)

TANOK. All the pros do it. Gotta show them I'm one of them.

(He takes a drag. They pass the cigarette back and forth a few times.)

You look tired. Long day?

ELENA. The longest.

And then Josefina was going on and on about her daughter's engagement, which I'm sure will send my mother into another one of her spirals about how I'm still single.

TANOK. My mother gave me the same speech over breakfast:

*(As **BEATRÍZ**.)* "Ay, Tanok! When are you going to find a nice girl and settle down?"

ELENA. *(As **PASTORA**.)* "Elena, are you trying to break my heart? I want to see you wear my veil on your wedding day."

(Beat.)

As if I didn't feel like a failure already.

Three years and I'm still cleaning at a university I could never afford myself.

It was only supposed to be temporary.

TANOK. It is.

My father booked a small tour to prep me for my corrida in Michoacán next month.

I'm telling him you're coming with us.

*(Off **ELENA**'s look.)* I want you there.

TANOK. Plus, I need someone to help me get ready. And you'd get to quit this shitty job.

I probably pay way better, anyway. It's win-win.

ELENA. So, instead of cleaning up after anonymous rich kids, I'm cleaning up after you?

TANOK. *(Jokingly.)* Who better? You already know what a mess I am.

(*She punches his arm.*)

ELENA. I don't know, Tanok. You always rope me into these big ideas that never work out – like that time you tried to sneak me into the corrida.

TANOK. Pastora spanked us so hard we couldn't sit for a week.

(*They laugh.*)

But now I can get you closer to the ring. You'll see everything, meet the right people. We can build on what we're doing here and find someone who wants to represent you.

ELENA. No one is going to take me seriously.

TANOK. So we'll make them.

I believe in you, Elena.

You've always been there for me. Let me do this for you.

(*He tosses her the capote.*)

ELENA. I can do it for myself, you know.

TANOK. I know you can, palomita.

El primer tercio.

(**TANOK** *moves to the opposite end of the picadero.*)

*(She gets into position. **TANOK** retrieves a pair of capped bull horns and holds them out at **ELENA**, ready to charge.)*

I'm going to come in on your right.

(He charges at her from his left and she does a beautiful pass.)

Not bad!

ELENA. I know.

*(They replicate the pass again. At the last minute, he switches directions and charges to her left. **ELENA** completes a successful pass but not as gracefully as before, and falls over. **TANOK** cracks up.)*

You came in from the *left*, cabrón!

TANOK. *(Laughing.)* I know!

ELENA. Changing direction on me at the last minute is a dick move!

TANOK. That's what the bull does. You're too comfortable!

(She flips him the bird.)

This is nothing. Last week, my father knocked me off my horse into the barrera. Grow a pair.

ELENA. You first.

TANOK. Ha, ha. Let's try it again, but this time close the distance between your feet a little more.

*(**TANOK** moves behind **ELENA** to instruct her, hand over hand.)*

The smaller the space, the easier the pass becomes. The magic is in the flourish, so just let your arms…

*(**TANOK**'s hands slowly slide down **ELENA**'s arms.)*

TANOK. ...do all the work.

*(**ELENA** closes her eyes, savoring his touch. A moment between the two of them. **ELENA** shakes it off, as **TANOK** moves away and takes his position across from her.)*

*(He charges **ELENA**. She makes a beautiful Veronica pass.)*

*(Throughout the rest of the scene, **TANOK** and **ELENA** continue to practice exercises for all three tercios, trading off positions so that the other can practice as the matador. [Note: **ELENA** and **TANOK** should always call for the bull to signal when they're ready to start the exercise.])*

ELENA. You want kids?

TANOK. What?

ELENA. Children. Offspring. Little toreros.

Do you want them?

TANOK. Don't you?

ELENA. I'm asking *you*.

*(**TANOK** is silent for a moment. Then:)*

TANOK. *(Sincerely.)* Yes.

But, someday, you know. Not...

Why?

ELENA. Just curious. We are getting older.

TANOK. We're only twenty-two.

ELENA. Even still. Maybe our moms are right.

Shouldn't we have a plan for our lives by now?

TANOK. We do. This.

ELENA. No, *you* have a plan, Tanok. You're actually living your dream. I'm...still sleeping.

TANOK. Not for long.

> (**TANOK** *finishes his final pass with a flourish.*)

Segundo Tercio.

> (**ELENA** *grabs two banderillas.* **TANOK** *moves to grab a wheelbarrow that holds a bale of hay and has bull horns on the front of it. In the center of the hay, there is a bright red circle to act as a target.*)

> (**ELENA** *calls the bull. They charge at one another. In one swift move,* **ELENA** *lands two banderillas in the hay, right on target – where the shoulder of the bull would be.*)

Do *you* want kids?

ELENA. I'm not sure.

TANOK. Don't all girls?

ELENA. Well, I'm not all girls.

> (**ELENA** *yanks out the banderillas. She resets, calls,* **TANOK** *charges her again.*)

And I'm not saying *no*, I'm just saying... I don't know.

> (*She lands the banderillas.*)

TANOK. Do you think it will make you happy?

ELENA. I think *this* makes me happy.

TANOK. Why can't you have both?

ELENA. Don't think you can have a double life when you have kids.

TANOK. Sure you can. Look at my father.

> (**TANOK** *yanks out the banderillas.* **ELENA** *grabs the wheelbarrow. They move to opposite ends of the picadero.*)

ELENA. What do you mean?

TANOK. You think he's been faithful to my mom this whole time?

ELENA. People are complicated, Tanok.

TANOK. Don't defend him.

ELENA. I'm not. I'm just saying things aren't always black and white.

> (**TANOK** *calls for the bull. They charge at one another.*)

TANOK. My mother has cried herself to sleep every night since I can remember.

> (**TANOK** *lands the banderillas, hard.*)

Don't really see a gray area there.

> (**ELENA** *and* **TANOK** *inspect the banderillas.*)

ELENA. You missed.

TANOK. A few centimeters off.

ELENA. Again.

> (*They reset.*)

TANOK. People have choices, Elena.

Like you – why don't *you* tell your mom that we do this every night?

(**TANOK** *lands the banderillas.*)

ELENA. You know why, Tanok. She barely likes that *you* do this.

Can you imagine if she found out that her only daughter wants to be a torera?

(*They switch positions.*)

TANOK. Is that so horrible?

ELENA. She only wants me to do what's expected of me.

(*They charge, and* **ELENA** *lands the banderillas right on target.*)

No surprises.

(**TANOK** *inspects her banderillas.*)

TANOK. Perfect.

You're much better than me – admit it.

ELENA. Oh, I *know* it.

Tercer Tercio.

(**TANOK** *resets the wheelbarrow, as* **ELENA** *grabs the sword and muleta. When ready,* **ELENA** *calls the bull to perform "La Faena." She completes four slow, graceful passes with the muleta, drawing the bull in closer and closer each time. She gets into position for the volapié – where the torera "hypnotizes" the bull with the muleta low to the ground and delivers a fatal blow with her sword.*)

TANOK. So, then why don't you just go for it?

Maybe if you stopped playing it safe, you could actually get somewhere and finally be able to have the life you always wanted.

(**ELENA** *stabs the bull.*)

ELENA. Who says I'm not living the way I want right now?

TANOK. Oh, come on. You know what I mean.

ELENA. No, I really don't. Please explain it to me.

What's so wrong with my life?

TANOK. Nothing really. It's just that every day you tell me how unhappy you are.

ELENA. Yeah, but I tell you that because you're my friend.

You're not supposed to use it against me.

TANOK. "Use it against –"

What are you talking about?

ELENA. My life is my life, and who are you to say that it can be better?

TANOK. Life can *always* be better. In the general sense.

ELENA. That's not what you meant.

TANOK. How do you know? Do you live in my brain?

ELENA. You don't know how hard it is to be a regular person, okay?

You just live in your bubble, and float above everything else.

TANOK. Are you on your period or something?

ELENA. Yes, as a matter of fact, I am.

At this very second, my uterine lining is crumbling out of me in big bloody globs.

You wanna see?

(*Beat.* **TANOK** *is really uncomfortable.*)

What's wrong, torero? You're not afraid of a little blood, are you?

(**ELENA** *starts to reach into her pants.* **TANOK**
grabs her hand to stop her.)

TANOK. Don't be crass, Elena.

ELENA. Oh, does my tasteless behavior offend you?

You think I'm beneath you, don't you?

TANOK. I don't.

ELENA. Did you ever think that I have to work twice as
hard as you?

That I have to literally fight for what I want?

I have to be "perfect" so I can prove that I deserve this
just as much as you do.

So, that *maybe one day* someone will look at me and
decide I'm good enough for them to take a chance on,
and not just be a sideshow.

And I can't tell my mother that this is what I want
because she has nothing in her life but me. My father
was killed in the ring saving yours, so how do I look her
in the face and tell her that her nightmare is my biggest
dream?

That is what I'm up against, Tanok.

You wanna talk about "playing it safe"?

The greatest bullfighters light the ring on fire with their
passion.

You've had everything handed to you, but I've never
seen you lose yourself in the dance.

TANOK. That's not fair. You know how hard I work.

ELENA. Then what are you so afraid of?

(**TANOK** *scoffs.*)

You're asking me to travel to the biggest bullrings in
the world to *clean up* after you, and you think you're
doing *me* a favor? Go fuck yourself.

TANOK. I'm just trying to help.

ELENA. I'm *better* than you. I should be where you are!

TANOK. Well, you're not.

No one is going to notice you without me.

ELENA. No one is going to notice me in the background stitching your clothes either.

I don't need a savior.

> (**DON RAFAEL** *enters undetected and observes the remainder of their conversation in silence.*)

TANOK. The only person who knows what you can really do is me.

You want to be where I am? Let's show Rafael.

ELENA. And risk losing his cochinito? That'll never happen.

TANOK. Then I'll talk to the promoters myself.

ELENA.

I don't need you to flash your father's money around town so that some managers will give me the time of day.	**TANOK.** Here we go again. Why are you so obsessed with my father's money, Elena?

ELENA. Because money is all that really matters in this world, Tanok! That's not an obsession, that's a fact. You are where you are because of your father. You don't know what it's like to *really* struggle.

TANOK. Neither do you! We grew up in the same house, ate the same food /

ELENA. That *my* mother cooked for *you*, in *your* house!

TANOK. You know it's not like that. You're a part of the family, Elena. You both are.

ELENA. Then why do we still eat in the kitchen?

(She waits for **TANOK** *to say something, but he doesn't know what to say.)*

If you can't even get me into the dining room, how the hell are you going to get me into the bullring?

(Silence.)

TANOK. Goodnight, Elena.

*(**TANOK** exits.)*

*(**ELENA** is alone. Frustrated, she takes the sword out of the bale of hay and walks to the other end of the ring. She swiftly turns and charges at it, and hits the target perfectly.)*

*(**DON RAFAEL** emerges from the shadows behind her.)*

DON RAFAEL. You really wound him up. Women have that effect on toreros.

You don't belong here.

ELENA. I came to watch Tanok. I was just leaving.

*(**ELENA** quickly grabs her things and moves to exit.)*

DON RAFAEL. Your form is quite good.

*(**ELENA** stops dead in her tracks.)*

Better than Tanok's. Did he teach you?

ELENA. We...teach each other, señor. He knows more than I do. Because of you.

*(**DON RAFAEL** removes the sword from the bale of hay and hands it to **ELENA**.)*

DON RAFAEL. The volapié. Show me again.

But this time, with your eyes closed.

Bullfighting isn't solely technique; it's also instinct.

Let's see if you have it.

*(**ELENA** takes the sword from **DON RAFAEL** and grabs the muleta.)*

(The air is heavy and somehow the space feels like it's getting smaller. Time slows.)

*(**ELENA** focuses on the bale of hay, "hypnotizing" it. She closes her eyes and breathes. Without hesitation, she makes a swift jab through where the nape of the bull's neck would be, right on target. She opens her eyes and stands frozen as **DON RAFAEL** inspects the bale. He runs his fingers over where the sword landed.)*

(Silence.)

*(**DON RAFAEL** looks at **ELENA** as if he's finally seeing her for the first time. It's unclear whether he is impressed or pissed.)*

It's late. Go home.

*(**ELENA** tentatively moves to hand him the sword and muleta, but he doesn't take it. She sets them down and scurries off.)*

*(**DON RAFAEL** stares at the bale, and then back towards where **ELENA** exited.)*

(Lights.)

2.2 Michoacán, México. 2002.
A Hotel Room. A Few Weeks Later.

(So late it's early.)

(A two-person after-party following Tanok's latest victory. **TANOK** *wears elements of his traje de luces, his chaquetilla is on the chair.* **ELENA** *wears the nicest dress she owns – it's simple but she looks stunning. Her shoes, rebozo, and purse are scattered around the room. They're both exhausted, yet glowing with spirited energy [post-prom or wedding vibes.])*

*(***ELENA** *and* **TANOK** *sing along to a song in the style of "Afila El Colmillo" by Mala Rodríguez and Titan on the radio and dance around the room, drinking tequila and sharing a cigarette.*[*] *They're feeling reeeeally good right about now.* **TANOK** *pours them a shot.)*

TANOK. For the bullfighting gods, wherever they may be!

ELENA & TANOK. Amen!

(They drink. **TANOK** *pours another, spills a little on* **ELENA***'s hand.)*

ELENA. Cuidado! That's good tequila you're spilling!

---

[*] A license to produce *Torera* does not include a performance license for "Afila El Colmillio" by Mala Rodríguez and Titan. The publisher and author suggest that the licensee contact ASCAP or BMI to ascertain the music publisher and contact such music publisher to license or acquire permission for performance of the song. If a license or permission is unattainable for "Afila El Colmillio," the licensee may not use the song in *Torera* but should create an original composition in a similar style or use a similar song in the public domain. For further information, please see the Music and Third-Party Materials Use Note on page iii.

TANOK. We'll order another bottle from room service.

It'll go on the bill, courtesy of the legendary Rafael Cárdenas.

ELENA. Sounds like a great way to get your ass kicked.

(They drink.)

TANOK. But drinking on someone else's tab makes the tequila smoother!

And I just made him a shitload of money, so he can't be mad at me for like, a week.

Come on, Elena, we're celebrating!

(He pours her another shot.)

ELENA. Ya, ya! No mas!

TANOK. *(Handing her the shot.)* To your health and happiness, palomita.

ELENA. *(Accepting it.)* Fuck that – to being the best there ever was!

TANOK. You've always been better at toasts.

(They raise their glasses.)

ELENA & TANOK. Arriba!

Abajo!

Al centro!

Pa'dentro!

(They clink their glasses and drink. It burns.)

TANOK. My father would be so offended if he saw this right now.

*(As **DON RAFAEL**.)* "Tanok! You *sip* tequila! You're not an American. *Sip* it!"

(They laugh. **ELENA** *pours them both a shot.)*

ELENA. To not being American.

ELENA & TANOK. Amen!

(They clink glasses, and take another shot.
ELENA *looks at* **TANOK**, *and smiles.)*

ELENA. You actually did it – the tail *and* ears!

TANOK. I thought I was going to piss myself.

ELENA. Ignacio de la Vega's career went straight to the top after his first tail and ears.

That's a lot of pressure. Sure you can handle it?

TANOK. Please, Elena. That's what men do.

We *handle* things.

ELENA. And women don't?

TANOK. You handle different things.

ELENA. Sucio! Every other thought men have is about what's between a woman's legs.

TANOK. That's not true.

ELENA. *(Pours herself another shot.)* Whenever we're at a bar and I have a conversation with a man, he thinks I'm only good for a fuck. And then when I tell him I want to be a torera, he has to prove how much stronger he is than me. If that's what womanhood is, I might as well settle down with someone like you.

*(***ELENA*** takes the shot.)*

TANOK. You'd be lucky to settle with someone like me. I'm a *rejoneador*.

Brave. Strong. Virile.

*(***TANOK*** winks at **ELENA***. She rolls her eyes.)*

TANOK. Did you see the how many handkerchiefs were waving?

The entire Plaza was swinging them back and forth, and back and forth...

Like I was walking through the clouds.

ELENA. You know, for twenty minutes, it was like we all forgot that the world outside is crumbling to pieces and you lifted us up with the flourish of your banderillas.

You're a hero, Tanok.

> *(It sinks in for* **TANOK***: he's finally made it – and he's terrified. He fiddles with his medallion. A moment of stillness.)*

Tanok... Are you OK?

TANOK. Never better.

Let's have another!

ELENA. *(Pouring* **TANOK** *a shot.)* We should slow down. You're going to be useless at practice tomorrow, and your father will blame me if you're anything less than perfect.

He already thinks I'm a bad influence on you.

> *(She drinks straight from the bottle.)*

TANOK. Of course he does. You're the worst.

ELENA. I'm going to punch you.

TANOK. Ha! You're a bullfighter, Elena, not a boxer.

ELENA. I could wipe the floor with you right now, if I wanted to.

The room is just spinning a little bit, so hang on.

> *(***ELENA** *and* **TANOK** *square off in a fighting position. She swings at him, but drunkenly misses, falls into his arms.)*

> (**TANOK** *starts to tickle her and they collapse onto the bed.* **ELENA** *struggles to escape as* **TANOK** *overpowers her with tickles.*)

ELENA.

(Laughing uncontrollably.)

No...nooo... St-st-st-o-ppppppp!! Please, Tanok! I'm – I'm – gonna throw up.

TANOK.

I thought you were going to punch me. What happened, huh? Huh? Huh????

ELENA. Truce?!

TANOK. Normally I wouldn't, but I need to lie down. Like right now.

Ughhh...

> (**TANOK** *falls to the bed.* **ELENA** *lays down next to him. They breathe in tandem, staring up at the ceiling.*)

ELENA. You're drunk.

TANOK. So are you.

ELENA. You're a really great guy...

I give you a lot of shit but that's only because you're my favorite person.

You know that, right?

TANOK. I know.

And despite all the obvious red flags, you're my favorite person, too.

I love you, Elena.

ELENA. I love you, too, Tanok.

> (**ELENA** *seizes the moment – leans in and kisses* **TANOK**, *tenderly. He pulls away, surprised. He kisses her again. The moment*

is sweet, but grows more passionate. **TANOK** *gently lays* **ELENA** *down on the bed. His hand begins to slide up her thigh, under her dress.)*

(Are they really about to do this?)

(Suddenly, **TANOK** *stops. He pulls himself off of* **ELENA**, *pulls her dress down for her.* **ELENA** *sits up. They're now both instantly sober.)*

TANOK. I'm sorry.

ELENA. Yeah, me too.

(Awkward silence.)

TANOK. I shouldn't have done that.

ELENA. Oh.

TANOK. No, no I – I just...wasn't expecting you to...

ELENA. Kiss you?

TANOK. Yeah...

You deserve something better than a drunken hook-up in a hotel room for your first time.

(Silence. **ELENA** *is mortified, vulnerable.)*

It *is* your first time, isn't it?

ELENA. *(Defensive.)* We're not kids anymore. I don't *have* to tell you everything.

(Beat.)

You're not the only one who can get lucky after a corrida. I'm desirable, too.

TANOK. You think I don't know that?

*(***ELENA*** gets up and grabs her stuff from all around the room.)*

Wait, Elena /

ELENA. I need to leave. // Like now.

TANOK. No, hold on a minute /

> (**ELENA** *grabs the chaquetilla off the chair and heads toward the door.*)

ELENA. I should get back to my room.

It's late – I have to finish sewing your chaquetilla.

TANOK. You don't have to leave.

ELENA. I *definitely* cannot stay here.

> (*He stands between her and the door.*)

Please move.

TANOK. No.

ELENA. Tanok, let me out of this room.

TANOK. Let's talk about this.

ELENA. Talk about what?

How stupid I feel?

How much I just want to disappear into the floor?

How standing in front of you right now is making my skin crawl?

> (**TANOK** *reaches for her.*)

TANOK. I'm sorry.

ELENA. Let me go.

> (**TANOK** *removes his hand.*)

Why did you stop?

> (**ELENA** *searches* **TANOK**'s *face for an answer but he doesn't know what to say. They stand together in silence for what feels like an eternity. Then:*)

ELENA. Let's just pretend this never happened.

> (**ELENA** *makes her way past* **TANOK** *and exits in a hurry.* **TANOK** *finally opens his mouth, as if to speak through the closed door, but nothing comes out. He slams his fist against the door.)*
>
> *(Lights.)*

2.3 La Plaza De Toros Mérida. 2002.
A Week Later.

(**TANOK** *confidently enters the bullring and salutes an adoring crowd.* **ELENA** *and* **DON RAFAEL** *look on. With bravado, he kneels before the bullpen to do the Porta Gayola.*)

(*The crowd goes silent. Burning anticipation.* **TANOK** *breathes deeply, then calls for the gate to open.*)

TANOK. Puerta!

(*The sound of the gate opening. More silence.*)

(*Then, it breaks – a rush of air and the scraping of hooves, as the bull explodes into the ring racing toward* **TANOK**.)

(**TANOK** *swiftly moves his capote in front of his body and above his head – but the bull does not follow; instead it crashes into* **TANOK**'s *body.*)

(*The horrific sound of stunned gasps from the crowd.*)

(*Blackout.*)

2.4 La Plaza De Toros Merída. 2002.
Infirmary.

(**ELENA**, **DON RAFAEL**, *and the* **ENFERMERA** *take* **TANOK** *into the infirmary on a rolling gurney.* **TANOK** *is unconscious and bleeding from his arm – he's been gored.* **ELENA** *holds his medallion in her hands.*)

DON RAFAEL. Mírame, Tanok – keep your eyes open!

ELENA. You're going to be okay, panzón... You're almost there...

ENFERMERA. Señor Cárdenas, I need you to wait outside.

DON RAFAEL.

The hell I am! Dónde está el doctor? I need to speak to him – Now.

ENFERMERA.

The horns went through your son's arm. We need space to work /

ELENA. Por favor, Enfermera – I have his medallion. Let me give it to him.

ENFERMERA. *Everyone* waits here, señorita. Lo siento.

(*The* **ENFERMERA** *disappears into the operating room, leaving* **DON RAFAEL** *and* **ELENA** *in the hallway alone. The faint sound of the crowd can still be heard in the distance.*)

(**ELENA** *stares at the doors ahead of her in shock.* **DON RAFAEL** *slams his fist against the wall and moves like a nervous tornado around the hallway.*)

DON RAFAEL. Puta madre!

ELENA. *(To herself.)* It's okay... He'll be okay... He always is...

DON RAFAEL. *(Accusatory.)* Whose idea was it to do the Porta Gayola?

(*Beat.*)

ELENA. Tanok needs the crowd to remember his name. Being on your knees in front of the gate says you are someone to be watched – respected.

The bull was *supposed* to veer to the right and follow the capote...

DON RAFAEL. *You* are not his trainer! I decide what's best for him. *Me.*

The only reason you're even here is because I *let* you be.

ELENA. Tanok wants me here.

DON RAFAEL. You've always been a distraction for him.

ELENA. He's never lost focus in a corrida. He always does everything you tell him to.

DON RAFAEL. Except today.

ELENA. Nothing fires up a crowd more than the Porta Gayola.

This *will* work, Don Rafael.

DON RAFAEL. You think just because you live in my house, watch toreros on TV, and talk to my son that you know more than I do?

You know how you become famous in this world? Live long enough for people to know who you are. Today, he's gored through the arm. But what about the next time?

This isn't some game you played in the orange grove. This is a dance with death.

> (**ELENA** *and* **DON RAFAEL***'s attention is pulled to the muffled sound of hooves scraping across the floor, followed by the roar of the crowd cheering on another torero.*)

(The joyous stamping of feet shakes the building. The audience has already moved on.)

DON RAFAEL. Every move you make has either a reward or a consequence, and it is very real.

I have invested too much in Tanok to let this be taken away from him.

ELENA. Taken from him, or taken from you?

DON RAFAEL. Who do you think you are, speaking to me like this?

You think you know so much, but you are no one.

You're an irritating footnote in Tanok's past and have no place in his future.

Yet you're pathetically hanging on.

Have you ever asked yourself why?

Because he will never see you as anything more than what you are: the help.

ELENA. With all due respect, Don Rafael – if you think Tanok is willing to give his heart to anyone except the bull, then you don't know your son as well as you think.

(The two face-off in tense silence for several moments, as more cheering from the crowd echoes around them.)

*(Then, suddenly, the infirmary doors swing open. **TANOK** walks toward them, physically weakened, but with determination nonetheless.)*

Tanok, you're alright!

*(**ELENA** rushes to embrace him, momentarily forgetting the injury to his arm. **TANOK** winces from the pain, but holds her close.)*

TANOK. Of course. I'm a bird. I'm invincible. I soar above everything – just like you, palomita.

> (**TANOK** *sees* **DON RAFAEL** *and moves toward him.*)

Señor, I can explain /

> (**DON RAFAEL** *slaps* **TANOK** *hard across the face. It's shocking.*)

I was just trying to /

DON RAFAEL. You could've been killed!

TANOK. I needed to stand out from the others.

DON RAFAEL. And you do – with your skill, not a stunt!

You are a *rejoneador*, Tanok. Your place is on a horse – closer to God, *above* everyone else.

TANOK. So, I'm supposed to let a less-skilled torero kill my bull for me after I've done all the work? Rejones rarely provide a quick death, and the crowd is always screaming for more. They've seen what I can do on horseback and adore me for it – they need to know that I can handle a sword and kill the bull. *Alone.*

Being a torero *and* a rejoneador was Ignacio de la Vega's calling card. It can be mine, too. I can be a great bullfighter, but you never give me the chance!

DON RAFAEL. Ingrato! You disrespect me.

You will be great when you deserve to be.

TANOK. I'm sorry I didn't tell you. But, I thought it would be better to beg for forgiveness than ask for your permission.

> (*A rhythmic clapping of the crowd is heard – they're calling for* **TANOK**'s *return.*)

I'm going back out there.

(They all know this is true – he has to.)

TANOK. Where's my capote?

ELENA. In the barrera.

Here – your medallion.

(She puts the medallion around his neck. He looks into her eyes.)

Don't stop now. You've come this far.

TANOK. We *both* have.

*(**TANOK** looks to **DON RAFAEL** for motivation, but he gives none.)*

*(**TANOK** is hurt, but starts to move toward the arena. **ELENA** follows. Then:)*

DON RAFAEL. Tanok...

You can never enjoy glory if you're dead. Entiendes?

*(**DON RAFAEL** hugs **TANOK**. **TANOK** melts into him. This is a rare but tender display of affection for two men trying to dominate this world.)*

You're an impulsive little shit, but you've got cojones.

ELENA. *(To **TANOK**.)* They're waiting for you.

(They all exit into the bullring.)

*(The audience cheers and applauds when they see **TANOK**. He greets them with arms wide open, shouts in triumph to rile them up. The crowd roars wildly in response.)*

(Lights.)

2.5 The Cárdenas Kitchen. 1987.
Fifteen Years Earlier.

(Very late.)

*(**PASTORA** sits at the kitchen table, folding the family's clothing. The radio plays a song in the style of "Hasta Que Te Conocí" by Juan Gabriel.* She sings along.)*

*(**DON RAFAEL** appears in the doorway behind her. He holds a bottle of tequila and a single glass behind his back.)*

DON RAFAEL. Pastora.

(She screams.)

PASTORA. Ay, Dios mío! Me asustaste!

DON RAFAEL. Perdón, perdón.

PASTORA.

How many times have I told you not to just sneak up like that? Shuffle your feet! Speak! Make *noise*!

DON RAFAEL.

It's late. I heard the radio playing. I came downstairs to see what you were doing.

*(**PASTORA** turns the radio off.)*

DON RAFAEL. You're a bundle of nerves.

---

* A license to produce *Torera* does not include a performance license for "Hasta Que Te Conocí" by Juan Gabriel. The publisher and author suggest that the licensee contact ASCAP or BMI to ascertain the music publisher and contact such music publisher to license or acquire permission for performance of the song. If a license or permission is unattainable for "Hasta Que Te Conocí," the licensee may not use the song in *Torera* but should create an original composition in a similar style or use a similar song in the public domain. For further information, please see the Music and Third-Party Materials Use Note on page iii.

PASTORA. Diablo.

DON RAFAEL. Miedosa.

Remember when we were kids and we would play hide-and-seek? I'd jump out of the closet and you'd be shaking in your chanclas.

PASTORA. You never did play fair.

DON RAFAEL. Was growing up with me so terrible?

PASTORA. Of all my childhood traumas, Rafael, you were by far the worst.

DON RAFAEL. But I'm so devastatingly handsome.

PASTORA. Cálmate, viejo.

  (Beat.)

Are you hungry? There's mole in that pot.

DON RAFAEL. Tequila?

  *(She gives him a knowing look. He gives it
  right back, with confidence.)*

(Indicating the clothes.) You know you have a whole room you can do this in.

PASTORA. That room is cold and completely devoid of feeling. I prefer the warmth of this table.

  *(**DON RAFAEL** runs his fingers across the
  divots in the wood.)*

DON RAFAEL. You and your dancing.

PASTORA. That was a long time ago.

DON RAFAEL. When things were simpler.

PASTORA. Age will do that – complicate things.

DON RAFAEL. Were we happier then?

PASTORA. Children are always happy because they don't know any better. With knowledge comes pain. It's the price of admission into adulthood.

DON RAFAEL. And here is the remedy.

(He sets the tequila down on the table. She pours for him.)

Where's *your* glass?

PASTORA. I'm not drinking.

DON RAFAEL. Drinking alone is a sin.

PASTORA. Then your fate was sealed long ago.

DON RAFAEL. *(Chuckles.)* Perhaps – but as my father told me, and his father before him, "Never turn down an opportunity to share a drink with a beautiful woman."

PASTORA. It's ill-fitting to drink with the master of the house.

DON RAFAEL. Since when are you one for tradition?

(She glares at him.)

PASTORA. Elena and Tanok start first grade tomorrow. I can't be up late.

(He offers his glass to her.)

DON RAFAEL. One sip. For me?

Por favor, Pastora. We are old friends.

*(**PASTORA** can't help but give a smile. She takes the glass from him.)*

PASTORA. To your health.

DON RAFAEL. No. To *yours*.

(She sips the tequila.)

PASTORA. *(Indifferent.)* It's okay.

DON RAFAEL. That's Reposado! It cost me a fortune!

(She passes him back the glass.)

PASTORA. I've always wondered what compels a man to spend his money on a small bottle of liquid when the rest of his country is starving.

DON RAFAEL. The success of this country doesn't depend on the drinking habits of a tired rejoneador.

PASTORA. No, its countrymen would rather scrounge their pesos together to see The Legendary Rafael Cárdenas in the bullring every Saturday afternoon.

Despite all their suffering, their poverty, you bring them hope – happiness.

Even if just for an instant.

But, are *you* happy, Rafael?

DON RAFAEL. When I bought this bottle I didn't realize I'd be cross-examined by a Zapatista.

*(**PASTORA** throws her hands in the air, starts clearing the table.)*

I'm kidding! I'm kidding!

"Am I happy?"

We're talking now, so yes.

*(Off **PASTORA**'s look.)*

You know I can't stand it when you tower over me. Sientate, mujer.

*(A moment. **PASTORA** sits across from **DON RAFAEL**.)*

PASTORA. What are you doing down here, Rafael?

DON RAFAEL. I told you, I heard –

PASTORA. Yes, but what are you *really* doing down here?

(*Beat.*)

DON RAFAEL. I don't have a good answer, I guess.

(**DON RAFAEL** *caresses the table.*)

This table has been through a lot of things.

(*A shared moment between them.*)

PASTORA. Do you remember that Noche Buena when your father went to Madrid for a corrida instead of coming home?

DON RAFAEL. He was always in Madrid.

PASTORA. But only once on Noche Buena. I remember because we were helping my mother make tamales. You were so upset, you were beating the masa with your fists.

(*Pointing to the table.*)

That's where *this* divot is from.

DON RAFAEL. Is it?

PASTORA. You said you never wanted to be like him.

DON RAFAEL. I was thirteen – I didn't *understand* him. What he did. Why the art is everything to a man like that. How much it provides, and how much it takes away.

PASTORA. And now?

DON RAFAEL. (*Gesturing to his house, his life.*) I know better.

PASTORA. Your father would be very proud, que en paz descanse.

Tanok and Beatríz are lucky to have you.

PASTORA. Elena and I are lucky to have you.

After Joaquín died, I didn't think I could go on, but there you were.

DON RAFAEL. Joaquín was my right hand.

That day…the bull was too wild… When it slammed into the barrera /

PASTORA. I don't need to relive it.

(The pain weighs heavily on them both.)

DON RAFAEL. Your husband saved my life.

And he didn't deserve to die like that.

PASTORA. No, he didn't.

*(**DON RAFAEL** drinks. A long silence.)*

DON RAFAEL. Pastora… I am…retiring.

*(Though **PASTORA** is stunned to hear this, there is a relief that washes over her. This goes unacknowledged by the two of them.)*

PASTORA. But, you're so young.

DON RAFAEL. My eyes are straining to see what lies ahead; I'm not as swift as I used to be.

My body's telling me it's time.

PASTORA. Does Beatríz know?

DON RAFAEL. You're the only person I've told.

(A moment.)

PASTORA. She'll be relieved.

DON RAFAEL. Maybe.

PASTORA. Of course she will. She'll get to see you more often.

And you'll be able to be there for Tanok, give him everything your father never gave you.

That's what you always wanted, right?

DON RAFAEL. ...I've never felt so terrified.

Rejoneo has been the driving force of my life. My only dream.

Without it – what will my dream be now?

> *(He drinks.)*

At least I'll always have the title.

The Legendary Rafael Cárdenas...hangs up his traje.

> *(He breathes deeply, staring into his empty glass. **PASTORA** places her hand on top of **DON RAFAEL**'s. Their eyes meet. He squeezes her hand in return. They release one another.)*

> *(Lights.)*

Tercer Tercio

3.1 Mexico City, México. Hotel Room.
2007. Twenty Years Later.

> (**ELENA** *helps* **TANOK** *dress into a spectacular traje de luces. His bare torso is a roadmap of scars.* **TANOK** *holds still as* **ELENA** *hems his trousers.*)

ELENA. Almost finished.

TANOK. We have time.

ELENA. I really like this traje on you, Tanok.

TANOK. It's a gift from the promoter.

ELENA. The silk must have cost a fortune, so try not to get slashed today.

TANOK. It's not by choice, believe me.

> (**ELENA** *cuts the thread with a pair of scissors. She adjusts the waistband.*)

ELENA. All done!

TANOK. Gracias.

> (**ELENA** *fastens the buttons on his shirt, and puts the chaquetilla on* **TANOK** *as he puts on his medallion.*)

ELENA. How did the sorting go?

TANOK. Amazing.

ELENA. Really? What are your lots?

TANOK. Fifty-nine and fourteen. The largest bulls in the entire corral.

It's perfect.

ELENA. What's your order?

TANOK. First and last.

ELENA. A bookend?! That's huge, Tanok!

TANOK. It is, isn't it?

ELENA. First and last at Plaza de Toros México – that's almost forty-two thousand people!

TANOK. It's the biggest corrida of my life.

ELENA. You'll do great – just don't /

ELENA & TANOK. Fuck up.

> (*They share a laugh.* **TANOK** *checks the time.*)

TANOK. Hey, in the closet, there's a box. Will you get it for me?

> (**ELENA** *moves to the closet and reveals a long white gift box, tied with a red silk ribbon. She brings it to the bed.*)

ELENA. Fancy. What's in it?

TANOK. Open it.

> (**ELENA** *tentatively opens the box. She gasps, and reveals a beautiful white and gold traje de luces. On the back of her chaquetilla is a beautiful embroidered dove.*)

ELENA. Wow. This is /

TANOK. Yours.

> (**ELENA** *looks at* **TANOK**.)

My entire career hangs on today. I'm not taking any chances.

I need the best of the best by my side and that's you.

Dance with me, Elena.

ELENA. I don't know what to say.

TANOK. Say "yes."

You've been on the sidelines for too long. It's time.

ELENA. But your father /

TANOK.   – is an observer. I'm a grown man. This is *my* call.

> (**TANOK** *moves* **ELENA** *toward the mirror and holds the traje de luces against her body.*)

You were born to do this. Show 'em how it's done.

> (**TANOK** *steps back and* **ELENA** *holds the suit close to her.*)

> (*Time slows, as the lights focus on* **ELENA**. *The suit shimmers.* **ELENA** *smiles.*)

> (*The scene transitions to the corrida. We are now in the bullring.*)

> (**DON RAFAEL** *observes from behind the burladero.*)

> (*A pasodoble plays as the paséillo begins.*[*] *The sound of an* **ANNOUNCER** *comes in over the loud speaker over the following action:*)

ANNOUNCER. Señoras y señores! Muchachos y muchachas! Bienvenidos a la corrida más grande del año aquí en la Plaza de Toros México. Los mejores toreros mostrarán su arte y habilidad, y serán premiados con gloria ante Dios y una multitud de cuarenta y dos mil almas! Con orgullo presentamos las festividades de hoy gracias a la generosidad de nuestros patrocinadores: Telcel, pan

---

[*] A license to produce *Torera* does not include a performance license for any third-party or copyrighted music. Licensees should create an original composition or use music in the public domain. For further information, please see the Music and Third-Party Materials Use Note on page iii.

Bimbo, Manzanita, Tecate, y el favorito de mi hijo, Choco Milk.

And now, let's welcome México's rising star, straight from the Yucatán Peninsula – a marvelous torero and rejoneador – the one, the only Tanok Cárdenas!

>   (**TANOK** *enters on foot, greeting the crowd. Thunderous applause. He signals for* **ELENA** *to join him. The applause grows louder as she greets them.*)

It appears that Tanok is not alone in the ring today. Who is this...woman? I'm hearing from my colleague that this is Tanok's apoderada, Elena María Ramírez. This is highly unusual. Maybe this Elena Ramírez is the next Lupita López or Cristina Sánchez.

Let's see if she has what it takes...

>   (**DON RAFAEL** *sees* **ELENA**, *rage spilling across his face. He moves toward the ring to pull her out, but the signal of the trumpets halt him. The first tercio is about to begin.*)

>   (**TANOK** *and* **ELENA** *make eye contact, nod to one another. They take their positions for the corrida.*)

>   (**TANOK** *grabs the capote, moves in front of the gate and gets on his knees to perform the Porta Gayola.*)

>   (*Tense silence.*)

TANOK. Puerta!

>   (*The sound of the gate opening, and the racing of hooves and snorting as the bull explodes into the ring with speed and ferocity.*)

>   (*The bull passes through the capote.*)

(Applause and cheers.)

*(**TANOK** stands, calls the bull, makes another clean pass, with a flourish.)*

*(**ELENA** comes in behind **TANOK**, as he passes the capote off to her. The ballet ensues and **ELENA** has the upper hand with each pass of the capote.)*

*(**ELENA** and **TANOK** each grab an end of the capote. They stand close together, opposite the bull. They call it, it charges. Together, they lift the capote up over the bull to make a clean double pass.)*

*(**ELENA** completes one more Veronica pass with the bull, as **TANOK** grabs two banderillas.)*

*(**TANOK** calls the bull, and they charge one another. He lands the banderillas with a flamboyant flourish. The crowd goes wild.)*

*(**TANOK** whistles loudly, and **ELENA** bursts into the center of the ring, two banderillas in hand, and charges at the bull.)*

(She jumps, landing them perfectly. The bull is angry, weakened.)

*(**TANOK** and **ELENA** turn to the President of the bullring, seated in the stands. They raise their hats in the air, as if to ask for permission to slay the bull. It's granted. Time for the final tercio.)*

*(**TANOK** looks to **ELENA**, nods. This is her chance. She smiles. Quickly, **ELENA** takes a muleta and an aluminum sword, performs*

"La Faena" displaying her skill and artistry. She is flawless. She makes four passes, each shorter and shorter, as she draws the bull closer and closer to her. It is finally subdued. The "moment of truth" has arrived.)

*(**ELENA** turns her back to get the killing sword and is met by the adoring crowd. She relishes in their applause and cheers, shows herself off with bravado.)*

*(Suddenly, the bull awakens and charges at **ELENA**.)*

Elena!

DON RAFAEL. Tanok, don't!

*(**ELENA** turns and sees the bull, just as **TANOK** steps in front of her and pushes her out of harm's way. He is gored and flung into the air like a rag-doll. A collective gasp from the crowd, followed by deafening silence.)*

No!

ELENA. Tanok!

*(**TANOK** lies bleeding on the ground, convulsing. **DON RAFAEL** rushes into the ring, rushes to **TANOK**. **ELENA** joins them. She pulls her white chaquetilla off her body to put pressure on the wound and it becomes drenched with blood. Her hands are shaking.)*

*(**TANOK** tries to speak.)*

No, no – don't talk. Lie still…

*(Panic sweeps across **ELENA** and **DON RAFAEL**'s faces, but they remain strong for **TANOK**.)*

DON RAFAEL. *(To* **ELENA***.)* Keep the pressure on until the
medics come.

> *(Calling out to the medics.)*

Dónde está el doctor?!

(To **TANOK***.)* It's just a scratch. You're going to make
it... You're going to make it...

> *(***DON RAFAEL** *cradles his son in his arms.*
> **TANOK***, weakened, reaches for his medallion.*
> *He rips it from his neck and puts it in*
> **ELENA***'s hand.)*

TANOK. *(Struggling.)* I'm okay... Finish it.

> *(***ELENA** *knows what has to happen. She leaps*
> *to her feet and grabs the muleta and killing*
> *sword. The dance ensues and she victoriously*
> *slays the bull.)*

> *(As the crowd goes wild,* **ELENA** *basks in the*
> *glory of her victory – a childhood dream*
> *realized.)*

> *(As the applause and joyous chanting grow*
> *louder and louder, the sound of medics,*
> **TANOK***'s last gasps for air, and* **DON**
> **RAFAEL***'s inconsolable weeping reverberates*
> *in the space.)*

DON RAFAEL. Tanok... Mijo...

> *(Time suspends itself.)*

> *(***ELENA** *is frozen, as* **TANOK** *lies dead in* **DON**
> **RAFAEL***'s arms.)*

> *(The crowd goes dark, as the lights close in*
> *on* **ELENA***. She stands alone, her hands and*
> *white traje soaked with Tanok's blood, like*

paint on a canvas. Her breathing grows ragged and intense, as she looks around the ring with grave uncertainty.)

ELENA. What have I done? What have I done?

(The scent of the oranges returns to the space, followed by the etherial sound of two children laughing and running through an orange grove.)

(Lights.)

3.2 The Cárdenas Kitchen. 2007.
A Week Later.

(Very late.)

*(***PASTORA***, in grief, sits at the kitchen table, caressing a favorite shirt of Tanok's – worn and full of love. She brings it to her face and inhales. She clutches it close to her chest, trying to keep him with her a little longer.)*

*(***ELENA*** enters from behind her.)*

ELENA. Mamá?

PASTORA. He had so many good shirts, but he loved this one.

I should have thrown this out years ago – look at all the holes.

(Beat.)

There's chicken on the stove.

ELENA. I'm not hungry.

*(***ELENA*** moves to sit with her mother, but ***PASTORA*** can't meet her gaze.)*

Mamá?

Please look at me.

*(***PASTORA*** looks at ***ELENA***.)*

Aren't you going to say something?

PASTORA. What would you like me to say, Elena?

ELENA. Something comforting...anything... I don't know.

(Silence.)

I keep replaying it over and over in my head.

It's all my fault, Mamá.

> (**ELENA** *expects her to object, but* **PASTORA** *says nothing.*)

You think that's true, don't you?

PASTORA. Here's what I *know*, Elena:

I raised you to be honest and you lied to me.

You told me you were going with Tanok to care for him.

Instead you're training in secret and pursuing something that would deliberately put you in danger.

Then I find out you step into a bullring – after everything I've told you about your father…

You had a responsibility to this family, to me.

I expected more of you because that is what this world expects of women like us.

> (**ELENA** *hangs her head.*)

I taught you to follow a certain path for your *protection* – one that would give you a long, happy life that you could be proud of.

ELENA. I *am* proud of my life.

Maybe it's the not one you want for me, but it's the one I choose.

PASTORA. Elena, I have always told you to know your place.

Why couldn't you just listen?

> (**ELENA** *exits.*)

> (**PASTORA** *melts into a kitchen chair. She leans her head on the table, listening.*)

> (*Lights.*)

3.3 The Cárdenas Kitchen. 2007.
That Same Night.

(Very late.)

*(**PASTORA** sits at the kitchen table, still looking at Tanok's worn shirt.)*

*(**DON RAFAEL** enters, visibly drunk, with a half-drunk bottle of tequila and an old photo album with childhood pictures of* **TANOK**. *He sits across from* **PASTORA**.*)*

PASTORA. What are you doing down here, Rafael?

DON RAFAEL. Do you remember this?

> *(**PASTORA** looks at the photograph. A birthday celebration. She smiles.)*

PASTORA. Tanok's sixth birthday. He wanted a dinosaur piñata but all we could find was a star.

He cried for hours because it wasn't what he promised his friends.

He always cared what other people would think, even then.

DON RAFAEL. *(Flipping through photos.)* I'm not in any of these.

PASTORA. No. You had a corrida in Mexico City that year.

DON RAFAEL. And the others?

> *(Silence.)*

PASTORA. Whatever you're looking for isn't in these photographs, Rafael.

Stop torturing yourself.

DON RAFAEL. I did everything in my power to make him the best. Taught him everything I know.

PASTORA. Beatríz is asleep. Go upstairs and join her.

DON RAFAEL. I'm not tired.

PASTORA. You're drunk.

DON RAFAEL. So what?

PASTORA. You need sleep.

DON RAFAEL. I said I'm not tired.

PASTORA. I know this feeling. When Joaquín died, it felt like someone had ripped me open from the inside. But I had to think of Elena /

DON RAFAEL. Don't speak her name to me!

He was my only son, and it's because of her that he's dead.

PASTORA. That's not fair.

DON RAFAEL. What kind of a mother raises a daughter like that?

PASTORA. The same kind that raised your son.

DON RAFAEL. After everything I've provided, this is how you repay me?

You destroyed my life.

PASTORA. Is that how you see it?

I have spent all my days cleaning up your messes and making you shine.

I have been beside you through your darkest moments, listened to you, consoled you, without a moment of gratitude or true reciprocation.

You *take*, Rafael.

Your hands may be polished but they're just as dirty as mine.

> *(****ELENA**** appears in the doorway behind them. She listens quietly, undetected by* **DON RAFAEL** *and* **PASTORA**.*)*

DON RAFAEL. What do you want from me, Pastora?

PASTORA. To be an honest man.

She needs to know.

DON RAFAEL. *(Hushed.)* We agreed to keep this quiet.

For Joaquín, for Beatríz.

PASTORA. Is that who we're *really* protecting?

Your daughter has been walking through the halls of your home for twenty eight years, and you've never once acknowledged her presence. Held her. Treated her the way a father is supposed to treat his child.

And you sit here going on about your guilt over missing Tanok's birthdays. What about Elena's?

DON RAFAEL. You're holding onto something that could never be, Pastora.

You need to let this go.

PASTORA. For whose sake, Rafael? It is exhausting carrying your secrets.

Is it so hard to admit that you loved me, even if just for a moment?

> *(****PASTORA**** waits for an answer, but* **DON RAFAEL** *can't give it. As she turns to leave,* **DON RAFAEL** *reaches out and gently takes hold of her hand. This is the first time they've touched in years. It's painful, bittersweet.)*

DON RAFAEL. I'm sorry.

PASTORA. *(Softly.)* Let me go.

> *(****DON RAFAEL**** releases her.)*

*(At the sound of footsteps from behind, they turn to see **ELENA**. They form a triangle, with the table of secrets between them.)*

*(No one knows what to say next. This world has shifted. **ELENA** races off.)*

*(**DON RAFAEL** and **PASTORA** are alone.)*

(Lights.)

3.4 The Picadero. 2007.
Immediately After the Previous Scene.

(**ELENA** *runs into the equitation hall. She leans against the barrera, trying to catch her breath. She kicks it repeatedly – perhaps it even splinters. She lets out the loudest, most painful, ungodly scream. It shakes the entire place.*)

(*She slowly sinks to the floor to ground herself.*)

(*After a moment,* **DON RAFAEL** *enters the ring, cautiously, keeping his distance from* **ELENA**. *Sensing him,* **ELENA** *lifts her head to meet his gaze. They face one another for a long, long time – a distorted mirror of one another.*)

(*The air is so thick with silence you could choke on it. A myriad of unspoken emotions spill across their faces. Throughout this wordless exchange, there should be some kind of acknowledgement of the tragic ripple effect this secret has had over the lives of this entire family – this can range from anger and betrayal, to hurt, to regret, and maybe, some small level of understanding, but not full-on forgiveness. That will take some time. Create space for this scene to be malleable, depending on how each actor is feeling.*)

(*As the scene draws to a close,* **DON RAFAEL** *opens his mouth to speak, but can't find the right words. So, he defers to the only shared language they know – bullfighting. He moves to grab the capote.* **ELENA** *stands. He tosses* *it to her, she catches it.* **DON RAFAEL** *reaches for the capped bull horns to charge her. They make several passes in silence, moving together in grief.)*

(The passes start small and gentle, but then become grander and more aggressive the more passes they complete. On the final pass, they stop to face one another, exhausted and out of breath.)

(For a moment, we wonder if this could be the start of something new for this family. But **ELENA** *forcefully throws the capote at* **DON RAFAEL** *and exits. He is alone.)*

(Blackout.)

3.5 Preparation Room, La Plaza De Toros Mérida. 2007.

(**ELENA** *is being dressed into her traje de luces by her* **GROOM** *– he adjusts her chaquetilla. She fastens Tanok's medallion behind her neck and touches the medallion tenderly.*)

(**ELENA** *stands before an altar with La Virgen de Macarena, clutching Tanok's silver medallion in her hand. She venerates before the ornate statue as she mouths her prayers.*)

(*The roar of the crowd outside is heard.*)

GROOM. Señorita, it's time.

(**ELENA** *nods. The* **GROOM** *drapes Elena's capote de paseo over her left arm, and exits.*)

(**ELENA** *breathes deeply.*)

ELENA. (*To herself.*) I'm a bird... I'm invincible... I soar above everything...

I'm a bird... I'm invincible... I soar above everything...

I'm a bird... I'm invincible... I soar above everything...

(*The doors swing open wide and bright sunlight floods the preparation room.*)

(*The crowd cheers. Deafening applause.*)

(*A pasodoble plays as* **ELENA** *fearlessly moves forward into the light.*)

(*Whiteout.*)

End of Play

www.ingramcontent.com/pod-product-compliance
Lightning Source LLC
Chambersburg PA
CBHW070636120726
47909CB00004B/1460